Seedling ™

GROWING WITH GOD

BIBLE

WRITTEN & ILLUSTRATED
BY THE DE VILLIERS FAMILY

WATERBROOK
PRESS

SEEDLING BIBLE
PUBLISHED BY WATERBROOK PRESS
12265 Oracle Boulevard, Suite 200
Colorado Springs, Colorado 80921
A division of Random House, Inc.

ISBN 1-4000-7121-6

Published in association with the literary agency of Alive Communications, Inc., 7680 Goddard Street, Suite 200, Colorado Springs, CO 80920.

Library of Congress Cataloging-in-Publication Data

Seedling Bible : sixteen favorite Bible stories for toddlers / written and illustrated by the de Villiers family.— 1st ed.
        p. cm. — (Seedling)
    ISBN 1-4000-7121-6
    1. Bible stories, English. I. Title. II. Series.
    BS551.3.V55 2005
    220.9'505—dc22

                            2005017753

Printed in Mexico
2005—First Edition

10 9 8 7 6 5 4 3 2 1

CONTENTS

God Makes the World
Genesis 1

First there was only darkness,
Then God said, "Let there be light!"
This light became the first day,
And the darkness the first night.

On day two, God made the sky.
On day three, the land and seas.
Then He made all things that grow—
The flowers, plants, and trees.

Seedling says:
Who makes
the flowers?

Can you show me the moon?

On the fourth day, God was busy
Making wonderful shiny lights.
The sun to shine in the day,
And the moon and stars at night.

On the fifth day,
God made birds—
Eagles, sparrows,
Ducks, and larks.
He filled the seas
With creatures—
Dolphins, whales,
And great white sharks.

On day six, God made animals,
From the small to the very big.
He made the little kitten,
The kangaroo, and the pig.

Now God was nearly finished,
With everything in His plan.
The last thing that He made,
Was a woman and a man.

By day seven God was done
Making everything He could.
So He rested from His work,
And said, "It is very GOOD!"

Growth Spurt

Who made all of the
flowers and animals?

13

Noah Builds a Big Boat

Genesis 6–8

When God looked around the world,
What He saw made Him very sad.
Noah and his family were good;
The rest of the people were bad.

So God went to Noah and asked,
"Will you build a great big boat?
Make it out of cypress wood,
Covered in sticky pitch to float."

Seedling says:
Have you ever seen a rainbow?

How many dogs can you see?

16

At last Noah finished the ark,
And the animals went aboard.
Noah took two of every kind,
As he was told by the Lord.

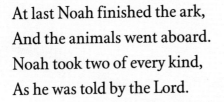

It rained for forty days and nights,
And water covered all the ground.
But floating in the big ark,
Noah's family was safe and sound.

Hurray, the rain finally stopped!
Noah let a dove fly free.
He knew the earth was dry and safe,
When it brought back a leaf off a tree.

"I will never do
this again," God said,
And He put a
rainbow up above,
To remind us of
This promise,
And His never-ending love.

Growth Spurt

What does it mean when
you see a rainbow?

God's Promise to Abraham
Genesis 12

Abraham listened when God spoke,
And he moved to a new land.
God promised, "You'll have a big family,
For this is what I've planned."

But Abraham was an old man;
His wife Sarah was old too.
They did not have any children,
So he asked God what he should do.

God took Abraham outside,
"Count all the stars you see.
I'll give you that many children,
If you will only trust in me."

Seedling says:
Have you ever made a promise?

That's a lot of shining stars!

So Abraham waited and waited—
He wondered if God forgot.
But God never breaks a promise,
Whether we think so or not.

When he was one hundred years old,
Sarah had Isaac, his son.
God fulfilled His promise,
Just as He's always done.

Growth Spurt

What did God promise
Abraham?

Joseph's Coat of Many Colors

Genesis 37

Joseph was the son of Jacob,
And he had eleven brothers.
But his Father loved him more
Than any of the others.

Jacob gave Joseph a coat,
The best he'd ever seen.
It had many wonderful colors —
Purple, yellow, red, and green.

Seedling says:
Has anyone ever
been mean to you?

Why are the brothers fighting?

When his brothers saw the coat,
They became, oh, so mad!
It was much better, by far,
Than any coat they'd ever had.

One day his father asked him,
"Please go to the fields and see
How your brothers are doing today,
Then hurry back to me."

When his brothers saw him coming,
They said, "Let's give him a scare,
We'll put him into a well,
And pretend to leave him there."

So when Joseph came to them,
The brothers took his coat away,
Then threw him in a well,
And left him there all day.

Some traders on camels came by.
"Let's sell him," the brothers said.
So they lifted him from the well,
And sent him to Egypt instead.

In Egypt, Joseph did well.
He became a very rich man.
Although his brothers did wrong,
It was all in God's perfect plan.

Growth Spurt

What was God's plan
for Joseph?

Baby Moses in the Basket
Exodus 2

Throughout the land of Egypt,
You could hear the mothers cry,
Because Pharaoh made a law
That all the baby boys must die.

But one young Hebrew mother
Looked at her sweet baby son,
"This child must be saved," she thought.
"Something must be done."

So she put him in a basket
To keep him warm and dry.
Then hid it in the river.
He didn't even cry!

Seedling says:
Have you ever found something?

What color is Moses's blanket?

The little basket floated along
Gently on the water.
Until later in the sunny day,
When it was found by Pharaoh's daughter.

She lifted up the basket,
"I wonder what it could be?"
Imagine her great surprise,
When she saw the tiny baby!

She took him to the palace,
So that he could live with her.
She named the baby Moses,
Because she'd found him
in the river.

Growth Spurt

How did Moses's mother
save him from harm?

The Parting of the Red Sea
Exodus 14

While they were living in Egypt,
The Hebrews worked hard all day.
Pharaoh forced them to make bricks,
Out of straw and clay.

When God heard His people's cries,
He said, "I must make a plan.
I need someone to help them,
And Moses is just the man."

Seedling says:

Do you ever need help?

Moses went to Pharaoh,
"God wants His people to go,"
But Pharaoh's heart was hard,
And he answered Moses, "NO!"

Can you show me the fire?

So God told His people to leave,
And He showed them the way,
With a pillar of fire at night,
And one of cloud by day.

At the Red Sea they made camp,
And were terrified to see
That very close behind them,
Was Pharaoh's whole army.

Moses said, "Don't be afraid,
Wait and see what God will do.
Today you'll see His power
Working to rescue you."

He held his hand over the sea,
And all night a mighty wind blew.
It pushed the seawater back,
And divided it in two.

The Hebrews hurried through the sea,
Walking safely on dry ground.
Then with a WHOOSH,
The water closed,
And Pharaoh's army drowned.

The people of Israel were safe,
They began to dance and sing,
"Praise God and His mighty power.
He saved us from a bad king."

Growth Spurt

How did God save
the Hebrews from
Pharoah's army?

David and Goliath
1 Samuel 17

This is the story of Goliath—
A giant who was nine feet tall.
And a shepherd boy named David,
Who wasn't very big at all.

David loved God with all his heart,
And always wanted to do right.
But Goliath did not love God,
And he only wanted to fight.

Each day Goliath would
Stand and shout
At the people of God's army.
"Send one of your soldiers out,
To come and fight with me!"

Seedling says:
Do you ever feel afraid?

Can you count all of the stones?

Everyone was afraid.
Only David said, "I will go.
My God is bigger than him,
And He'll help me, this I know."

David had five stones and a sling.
Goliath had a spear and sword.
But David looked at him and said,
"I come in the name of the Lord."

David slung a stone at the giant.
Whack! It hit him in the head.
Hurray, hurray, God's people cheered,
For Goliath the giant was dead!

We learn from this great story,
There is nothing you can't do.
If you love God with all your heart,
And trust Him to care for you.

Growth Spurt

Who will help you when
you feel afraid?

Daniel in the Lions' Den
Daniel 6

Daniel always trusted God,
And prayed to Him each day.
So God made Daniel very wise,
And blessed him in every way.

Some of the men did not like Daniel.
He was in charge of everything.
So they made an evil plan,
And took it to the king.

"Oh, King, let's make a law
To let the people know,
That everyone must worship you,
Or into the lions' den they'll go."

Seedling says:
Have you ever been treated unfairly?

What sound does a lion make?

Now, when Daniel heard the unfair law,
He knew he could not obey.
He would still worship God,
And pray three times a day.

The bad men saw him praying,
And went to the king again,
"We saw Daniel worshipping God,
Throw him in the lions' den."

It was dark down in the lions' den,
But Daniel was not afraid.
He got down on his knees,
And to God, for help he prayed.

God sent a mighty angel
To shut the lions' mouths tight,
And Daniel slept quite safely,
All throughout the night.

Now early the next morning,
The king got a big surprise,
When they opened up the den,
And Daniel was still alive.

This made the king so happy,
That he made a new decree.
From this day on, forever,
All must worship God only.

Growth Spurt

What did God do to
protect Daniel?

Jonah and the Big Fish
Jonah

Jonah, the prophet, told people
What God wanted them to know.
One day God said to him,
"To Nineveh you must go."

But Jonah was too afraid
Those people were not good.
So he decided to run away,
As far from God as he could.

He ran down to the seaport,
And went aboard a ship
That was sailing far out to sea,
To try to give God the slip.

Seedling says:

Have you ever been disobedient?

Can you find Jonah in the fish?

But God knew where he was—
Jonah was not able to hide.
God sent such a mighty storm,
That the sailors were terrified.

When they heard what Jonah had done,
The sailors threw him in the sea.
The wind and the waves died down,
And the storm cleared up quickly.

Poor Jonah was in the water,
Sinking down and down and down,
But God had made a plan,
So that Jonah would not drown.

A large fish swallowed Jonah—
He was stuck in its big belly.
He cried to God for help.
It was getting rather smelly!

"I'll do what you asked," Jonah said.
God heard his desperate plea.
After three days and three nights,
The fish spit him up safely.

Jonah hurried on to Nineveh
To tell them God was mad.
Then everyone changed their ways,
And did good instead of bad.

Growth Spurt

What happened when Jonah did what God told him to do?

The First Christmas
Luke 2

An angel came to Mary,
Because she was the chosen one.
Mary would soon have a baby,
And He would be God's only son.

Mary and her husband, Joseph, went
To the town of Bethlehem.
But when they finally arrived,
There wasn't room for them.

Seedling says:

Have you ever
been given a gift?

What is your favorite song?

A very kind innkeeper
Let them sleep in his cow stall.
There the little baby was born,
Who would become King of all.

In the fields outside the town,
Were shepherds with their sheep.
But on that special night,
They could not get to sleep.

There was a sudden flash of light!
And right before their eyes,
Hundreds of singing angels
Filled the nighttime skies.

"Go to Bethlehem," they said.
The shepherds hurried on their way.
There they found a little baby,
In a manger filled with hay.

Mary smiled and whispered softly,
"Jesus is this baby's name,
And now that He is born,
Things will never be the same."

Growth Spurt

Why is Christmas special?

Jesus Feeds 5,000 People
John 6

People came from everywhere
To hear what Jesus would say.
They loved to listen to Him,
And followed Him all day.

The disciples went to Jesus,
"What can we do?" they said.
"Everyone here is hungry,
And we don't have any bread."

grrr
grumble
rumble

Seedling says:
Do you like
to share?

Fish is my favorite, yummy!

A boy stepped from the crowd,
"You can have my lunch, if you wish.
It's only five small loaves of bread,
And two tiny little fish."

"Just five loaves and two fish?"
The disciples asked, with a frown.
But Jesus smiled and said,
"Please have everyone sit down."

Then Jesus looked
Up to heaven,
And said a
Thankful prayer.
When He handed
Out the food,
There was plenty
For all to share.

The disciples were amazed,
Five thousand people had been fed!
They even filled twelve baskets
With left over scraps of bread.

Growth Spurt

Is God happy when
you share?

70

Jesus and the Children
Mark 10

As Jesus went from town to town,
He didn't get much rest.
Mothers brought their children to Him,
With hopes that they would be blessed.

The disciples came along,
And chased the children away.
"Don't bother Jesus," they scolded,
"He's far too busy today."

Seedling says:
Do you ever feel
left out?

Do you like to get lots of hugs?

When Jesus saw what happened,
He took a child by the hand,
And said to the disciples,
"Why can't you understand?"

My kingdom belongs to children,
So please don't stand in their way.
If you believe like a child does,
Then you'll go to heaven one day.

Growth Spurt

Does Jesus have time
for you?

The First Easter
Luke 23–24

A shocking thing happened.
Angry soldiers took Jesus away.
He was put on a cross and He died—
His followers were very sad that day.

Jesus's friends took His body,
And laid Him in a cave alone.
To close the entrance to His tomb,
They placed a heavy stone.

Seedling says:
Why is the cross important?

Can you see anything inside?

It was early Sunday morning and
His friends came back to His grave.
What a surprise they found!
The stone was removed from the cave!

When they looked into the tomb,
His friends were alarmed to see
That Jesus was not inside,
And the grave was quite empty!

Two angels appeared to them,
"We have good news," they said,
"HE HAS RISEN, HE IS ALIVE!
Jesus is no longer dead."

Jesus visited them
When the disciples
Were all together.
"Believe in me," He said,
"And you will live forever."

Growth
Spurt

What happens if you
believe in Jesus?

Paul's Journey

Acts 9

There once was a very mean man
Who did not love God at all.
He wanted to hurt the Christians.
This mean man's name was Paul.

Paul went up to Damascus,
To find all of the Christians he could.
He wanted to take them to jail.
God said, "This is NOT GOOD!"

Seedling says: Have you ever been on a journey?

As he walked along the road,
There was a flash of light
That came from heaven above,
And Paul fell down with fright.

Ouch! What happened to Paul?

A voice from heaven asked,
"Why do you persecute me?
Get up, go to the city,
And wait there patiently."

Paul's friends were all dumbstruck.
They could hear only the sound
Of a voice from up above—
There was no one else around.

His friends helped him stand up,
And they were dismayed to find
That he couldn't see a thing—
Paul was completely blind!

So they led him by the hand
To a house on a street called Straight
And for three days and nights,
All he could do was wait.

Then God said to Ananias,
"Go and visit Paul for me.
Place your hands over his eyes,
And he will be able to see!"

Now Paul was a changed man.
He loved God in every way.
He went from place to place,
Teaching people how to pray.

Growth Spurt

How did Paul change?

Paul and Silas in Jail
Acts 16

Paul and Silas traveled around,
And everywhere they went,
They told about being saved
When you believe and you repent.

People were mad
at the apostles' words.
They grew angry and protested.
They dragged Paul and
Silas to the judge,
And had the men arrested.

Paul and Silas were put in jail;
They did not try to fight.
But sang hymns and prayed to God
In the middle of the night.

Seedling says: Have you ever been in trouble?

How many keys can you see?

The earth began to tremble,
With a rumble and a roar
That shook the jailhouse walls,
And opened every door.

The keeper was amazed
The prisoners hadn't run away!
So he went to Paul and asked,
"How can I be saved today?"

"Believe in Jesus," Paul replied,
"Trust God to care for you.
Then you'll be saved from sin,
And you'll go to heaven too."

Growth Spurt

What happened after God
sent the earthquake?

Jesus Is Coming Back
Revelation

As John was praying one day,
He heard a trumpet sound.
He couldn't believe what he saw
When he turned himself around.

Jesus was standing there,
His hair all blazing white.
In His hand were seven stars,
And His face was shining bright.

Then Jesus said to John,
"There is nothing for you to fear.
I want you to write down
Everything you see and hear."

Seedling says:
Have you ever thought about heaven?

On that amazing day,
John saw so many things.
Like God's new heaven and earth,
With Jesus as King of kings.

But of all the things John saw,
The most important
Lesson he learned
Was that sometime very soon,
To earth, Jesus will return.

Jesus is coming SOON!
What a wonderful day that will be.
Those that believe in Him
Will live for eternity!

Growth Spurt

What will happen when
Jesus returns?

About the Authors and Illustrators

Robbie de Villiers is a graphic designer whose work has earned international recognition, including two Clio Awards for excellence in advertising and nineteen International Clio nominations. His design company has provided service to several Fortune 500 clients as well as high-profile Christian organizations. Robbie has created the Seedling and Sprout books with his wife, Dianne; his daughter, Michelle de Villiers-Newton; and his son, PJ. Originally from South Africa, the de Villiers family now lives in Connecticut.

For more fun, visit the Seedling and Sprout Web site at:
www.seedlingandsprout.com

Look out for the *Sprout Bible* & Storybooks!

PEEKABOO, I Love You

SUPER DUPER Sundae Sleepover

Now available! Seedling Storybooks